To my wonderful Janie, who is unforgettable
—L.W.

For Juli, with all my love
—J.W.

www.randomhouse.com/kids

Library of Congress Cataloging-in-Publication Data
Weinberg, Larry.
The Forgetful bears help Santa / by Larry Weinberg ; illustrated by Jason Wolff.
p. cm.
SUMMARY: When Mr. Forgetful sees Santa's clothes and reindeer,
he forgets who he is and delivers toys to children.
ISBN 0-375-82291-7 (trade) — ISBN 0-375-92291-1 (lib. bdg.)
1. Santa Claus—Juvenile fiction. [1. Santa Claus—Fiction. 2. Memory—Fiction.
3. Christmas—Fiction. 4. Bears—Fiction.] I. Wolff, Jason, ill. II. Title.
PZ7.W4362 Foo 2002   [E]—dc21   2001033084

Printed in the United States of America
September 2002
10 9 8 7 6 5 4 3 2 1
RANDOM HOUSE and colophon are registered trademarks of Random House, Inc.

The illustrations for this book were created with acrylic.

The FORGETFUL BEARS HELP SANTA

by Larry Weinberg

illustrated by Jason Wolff

Random House 🏠 New York

'Twas the night before Christmas, when all through the house . . . not a Forgetful remembered it was the night before Christmas.

Everyone was in bed and fast asleep when suddenly there was a loud noise. Mrs. Forgetful opened her eyes. She shook her husband. "Wake up!" she whispered. "I think there's a burglar downstairs!"

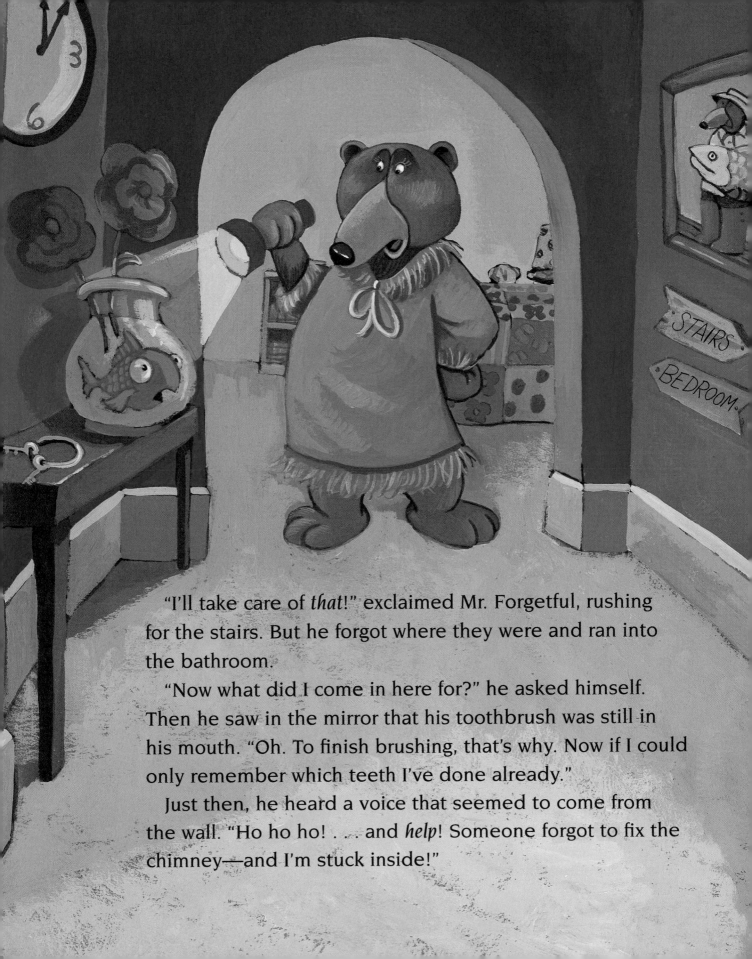

STAIRS

BEDROOM

"I'll take care of *that*!" exclaimed Mr. Forgetful, rushing for the stairs. But he forgot where they were and ran into the bathroom.

"Now what did I come in here for?" he asked himself. Then he saw in the mirror that his toothbrush was still in his mouth. "Oh. To finish brushing, that's why. Now if I could only remember which teeth I've done already."

Just then, he heard a voice that seemed to come from the wall. "Ho ho ho! . . . and *help*! Someone forgot to fix the chimney—and I'm stuck inside!"

"Brushing can wait!" cried Mr. Forgetful, running out of the room. He turned on the lights and found the stairs. "There you are, you crook!" he yelled as he ran down. "I've got you now!"

"Will you please take your paws off me!" shouted Grandpa Forgetful. "I am your father!"

"Oh. Are you really?"

"Yes. But I thought I heard you calling that you were stuck in the chimney."

"Hmm. I wonder why I did that," said Mr. Forgetful, scratching his head. "Well, anyway, I'm all right now."

"But *I'm* not! Ho ho ho!" cried a voice from the fireplace.

Looking up the chimney, Mr. Forgetful saw a man with a
long white beard and a bright red suit. He wagged his finger
at the man. "Shame on you! Sneaking into our house like that."

   "Oh, I wasn't sneaking. Well . . . yes, I was . . . ho ho ho! But
for a good reason."

Mrs. Forgetful came into the room. "Some good reason!" she exclaimed. "You dropped this bag full of toys when you tried to get away. Imagine—taking things from *children*!"

"But I wasn't taking them, dear madam. I was *bringing* them! Ho ho ho!"

"You can 'ho ho ho' all you want, but you won't fool us," insisted Grandpa Forgetful. "We know perfectly well that *Santa Claus* is the only one who ever climbs down chimneys bringing gifts. And he never arrives on the Fourth of July!"

"That's very true," sighed the man in the chimney. "But it doesn't *snow* on the Fourth of July, either."

The Forgetfuls all looked out the window. "So that's what that stuff is," said Mrs. Forgetful. "I couldn't imagine why it was so *dusty* outside."

"*Merry Christmas, one and all! Now, would you get me down, please?*"

The Forgetfuls tugged and pulled until Santa was free.

"Thank you very much," said Santa. "Here are gifts for
Sally and Tommy. And now I must be on my way."

"But just look at your clothes," said Mrs. Forgetful.
"They're filthy! You won't set *one* foot out of this house
until you're neat and clean."

So Santa Claus put on Mr. Forgetful's bathrobe. "I'm really in a very big hurry," he said as he gave his dirty red suit to Mr. Forgetful. "Will you promise to wash this quickly?"

"Absolutely!" Racing down to the basement, Mr. Forgetful popped Santa's suit into the washing machine. Then he waited right there until it was washed and dried.

"I kept my promise," he told himself proudly. "But who did I make it to?"

Coming up the stairs, he noticed there was someone sitting in the kitchen with Mrs. Forgetful.

"I thought that was *my* robe," said Mr. Forgetful to himself. "But if it belongs to him, then *these* clothes must be mine." And he put them on.

Just then, Mr. Forgetful heard some banging noises coming from the roof. He went up to have a look—and saw a big sleigh filled with presents. Hitched to the sleigh were eight reindeer, snorting and stomping because they wanted to be on their way.

Mr. Forgetful looked at them, then at his red suit. "Well,
I won't keep you waiting a moment longer!" he cried. And
jumping into the sleigh, he shouted, "On, Grumpy! On, Sneezy!
On, Dopey! On, Bashful!"

He couldn't understand why the reindeer didn't move.

Suddenly two windows flew open, and two little heads popped out. "Look!" Sally yelled to her brother. "It's Dad!"

The children threw on their coats and were up on the roof in a flash.

Mr. Forgetful was glad to see them. "Does anybody remember how to *start* this thing?"

"Sure, Dad!" Tommy picked up the reins and shouted, "On, Batman! On, Robin! On—"

"No, Tommy," cried his sister. "Those are not their names!"

"Then what are they?"

"Hickory! And Dickory! And Dock!"

The reindeer rolled their eyes and groaned.

"We'll just have to walk," said Mr. Forgetful. They picked up all the presents they could carry, and set off.

As they went along, Tommy pointed to a house. "Dad, I know who lives there. It's . . . it's . . . oh, what's his name?"

"Hmm. I see it says 'O'Reilly' on the mailbox. But there's no 'O'Whatshisname.'"

"Sally, you know who I mean! He's the biggest, meanest kid in the whole school."

"He sure *is* mean. He's always taking my dolls and throwing them."

Mr. Forgetful's eyes opened wide. "He likes dolls? Then I guess this must be for him." He carried a dollhouse in through one of the windows.

Soon they were all rushing in and out of houses. "Let's see! The red box goes to the boy in the blue house. No, the blue box goes to the girl in the red house! No! That's not it!"

After a while, they ran out of gifts. "But there's a boy in that new house," said Sally. "He needs a present, too."

"Let's go home and bring him some of *our* toys!" suggested Tommy. "But in case he wakes up, let's leave him a note saying that Santa will be back."

"I'll do it," said Sally. But when she went into the house, the television was on. So she sat down to watch.

When she didn't come back, Tommy opened one of the windows. *"Psssst! Pssst!"* he called softly. "Where are you?"

"Right here!" said the little boy, waking up. "I'm Justin. Who are you?"

Meanwhile, back at the Forgetfuls' house, Santa Claus was waiting in the kitchen. It was already morning!

"Why is it taking so long to clean my clothes?"

Mrs. Forgetful went to find out and discovered that Santa's suit was gone. So were her husband and children.

"Christmas is ruined! Ruined!" cried Santa.

"No, it isn't!" shouted Grandpa, hurrying out of the house. "We'll find them, or my name isn't . . . or my name isn't . . ." He jumped into the car and started to drive away.

"Wait! You forgot *us!*" Santa and Mrs. Forgetful yelled until Grandpa came back.

The car whizzed through town. "Stop!" said Santa. "That's one of the houses I go to."

He ran to the door and knocked very hard.
A huge bull answered it. *"WELL?"*

"Uh, excuse me, sir. My name is Santa Claus. However, I'm afraid somebody else is wearing my clothes and going around with toys. But here's my big belly, and here's my white beard. Do you want to hear my ho-ho-ho?"

"No, I don't!" the bull roared. "Not if you're trying to take back that dollhouse my son just got!"

"He got the *dollhouse*?"

"Yes—he loves it. And he's going to keep it!"

"Well, uh . . . of course," said Santa. "Merry Christmas." He walked away, scratching his head. "But then who got the football equipment I was going to leave here?"

Suddenly a football whizzed through an open door across the street.

"Mister! Catch!" Out burst a girl in a football uniform.

"Can that be you, Jennifer, under all that padding?"

"Why, sure it's me! But who are you?"

"I'm Santa. Now listen, child. I know you wanted a different gift, but we had a little problem, and—"

"Oh, who cares about that!" cried the girl, throwing her arms around him. "This is so much better than the silly old dollhouse I asked for."

"I'm so confused," moaned Santa as he drove off again with Grandpa and Mrs. Forgetful.

They were just driving around the corner when Mrs. Forgetful pointed to a window. "Isn't that fellow inside wearing your suit?" she asked.

"It's your husband!" cried Santa. "Stop right here!" And they all hurried into the house.

Santa was pretty upset with Mr. Forgetful. "Can I *please* have my clothes back?" he asked.

"Are they yours?" said Mr. Forgetful. "Well, I do beg your pardon. But you really shouldn't go leaving these things around, you know."

"Oh, Santa!" cried Justin. "Thank you for giving me the *perfect* Christmas present." He took Sally and Tommy by the hand. "My two new friends!"

Then Justin's mother made a big Christmas breakfast. And they all sang and laughed and had a wonderful time—which they never forgot!